BONUS PREQUEL NOVELETTE

NOT THE QUIET FRENCH KID

an origin story from the Fashion and Fiends series

ANGEL ACKERMAN

To Eva
part one
In Honor of her Graduation from High School

JULES SHOVED HIS BROTHER, Benji, perhaps harder than he intended, perhaps not. Benji matched him in height and weight so Jules couldn't reach over him or even around him to swap his books in the locker the school forced them to share. Benji's head of thick black hair blocked every attempt Jules made to put his British lit book away and grab his gym bag.

"What the hell are you doing, Benji?" Jules barked in French.

"It's Louis, Jules. Benji is a kid's name, or a dog's name," Benji responded in English.

"Whatever," Jules said, also in English, with the same tone he'd heard the American kids use. "It's not going to stick. Come on! Let me in! Your chemistry class is right here and I need to traverse the entire building!"

"Traverse?" Benji repeated. "No wonder you're having a hard time fitting in."

"I'm going to be late for Home Ec, again! And that *espèce de salope* has no more sympathy for my new kid routine."

Benji snickered and moved to the side. Jules slapped him in the back of the skull.

"It's not funny," Jules snapped as he seized his backpack from the hook.

"Be grateful that French class fit into your schedule, or you could be sewing and cooking with the girls," Jules said.

Jules jogged down the hall, quasi-backwards, determined to reach his next class on time.

"Face it, Jules. You like the cooking," Benji remarked. "Hey, look out!"

And then Jules hit something.

"Hey, watch it!" the something said.

Jules turned. The object he hit pivoted.

"Well, Jewel. Excuse me, Mr. Wee-Wee Poo-Poo."

Jules exhaled. "Sorry, Bobby. I've got to get to Home Ec."

Bobby Lincoln, a football player with a crew cut and no neck, laughed. He poked Jules in the chest.

"Gonna make me something to eat, Mr. Wee-Wee?"

"Bobby, I really don't have time for this…"

Jules maneuvered around him, but Bobby stepped squarely into Jules' path.

"First you have to suck my dick."

"Find someone else to play fireman," Jules said as he barreled past Bobby, their shoulders slamming together. The bell rang. *Putain.*

Jules broke into a run.

"This isn't over, French boy," Bobby yelled.

"It never is," Jules muttered as he raced toward the front of the building.

Mrs. Diefenderfer had already distributed the recipe for French toast casserole when Jules arrived, breathless and skidding to a stop.

"Nice of you to join us, Jules," she said, whipping a sheet off her pile as he continued into the classroom.

"Thank you, Ma'am," Jules said as he accepted the paper.

"Jules, the next time you're late I'm going to give you a detention."

"*Oui, Madame,*" Jules replied without thinking.

The class erupted in giggles. Jules joined his group: Mindy, Dorothy and Samantha. Dorothy smiled when he dropped his backpack on the floor.

"I already preheated the oven," she whispered.

He nodded. Stupid graduation requirements, he fumed in his head. The guidance office had insisted that he and Benji take a French class to satisfy their foreign language requirement. Never mind that French was their native language. That didn't matter to the guidance counselor. Since he and his brother obviously spoke English, French qualified as a foreign language. If they could pass French IV, they could satisfy the requirement. As a senior, Benji could fit the class in his schedule with no problem. Somehow French IV and the typical sophomore line-up of biology, British lit and Algebra II left him room for two other electives, but enrollment numbers and scheduling conflicts landed him in home economics and woodshop.

He and Samantha broke bread into pieces, arranging them in the dish according to the directions. His peers whipped eggs and milk together. Mindy measured the nutmeg. The aroma, sweet and yet delicately spicy, wafted from the liquid mixture and brought out the richness of the milk. Mindy sprinkled it slowly from the small plastic spoon. She went to dump the remaining grains and Jules grabbed the spoon from her hand.

"No," he said. "You have it perfect."

"But the recipe says—"

"I don't care what the recipe says. My nose says it's perfect," Jules commanded.

Samantha sneered.

"Why do you think you're above following the directions? Because it's French toast?" Samantha said.

"There is nothing French about this," Jules said.

The teacher stood at the edge of their work center.

"Is there a problem?" she asked. "Jules, are you causing a problem?"

"No, Ma'am."

Mrs. Diefenderfer circulated to the other groups. Jules and Samantha finished placing the bread in the Pyrex rectangle, Dorothy poured the egg mix over it, and Mindy added blueberries. At that point, they covered the dish, labeled it with their group number and placed it in the refrigerator. They would bake it tomorrow.

After Home Ec, he dashed to gym where the Bobby Lincoln-wanna-bes kept tripping him during a game of basketball, not a hard feat when the victim resembles a six-foot-two wispy tree. After he peeled himself off the floor for the thirty-second time and nailed a basket, Coach Klide blew his whistle. Mathematics remained the only thing left to survive today.

When Jules reached his locker, Benji was not there. He stuffed his books inside and grabbed what he needed. Slamming the locker, Jules nearly bumped into Taylor, the all-American, blonde, blue-eyed boy that epitomized how Jules had imagined all California teenagers. Or maybe he'd watched too many surfer movies.

"Hey, Jules, right?" Taylor greeted him.

Taylor wrapped his arm around Jules' shoulder, and Jules realized Taylor wasn't that much shorter than him. Other than his brother, not many people in high school stood six feet tall.

"I may be taking advantage of you, but I'm desperate," the boy said. "Can you help me study French? I know, it's uncool to ask you when you don't even know me. If you can help me out with subjective future imperfect whatever, I will reward you with Mountain Dew and Street Fighter II."

"Are you serious?" Jules said as they moved toward the classroom.

"Deadly, man. Did I mention I live next door to Laura Portersmith?"

Laura Portersmith looked like a modern Brigitte Bardot, endless waves of blond hair, dark eyes, full lips and even fuller tits, and small proportions, including a tiny waist, that made him want to scoop her into his arms and run away with her.

"So?" Jules replied.

"I know when she gets home from cheering practice. That's when she takes a shower and runs around her room in a towel."

"How bad are you at French?"

"Is that a deal-breaker? Help me reach C level, that's all I'm asking."

"Street Fighter II?" Jules replied as he slipped into his seat.

Taylor nodded. He headed towards his seat two rows up and a row over.

"My mom's making meatloaf," Taylor said as he dropped his books on his desk. "You can call your mom from my house."

His brother could trek to the elementary school by himself to retrieve their sister, Minette. As long as he was home by seven to help prepare dinner, no one would care.

"Okay," Jules said.

Taylor sat down. "But what I don't get is this… You're French, right? But you don't sound French."

The bell rang. The teacher stepped to the chalkboard.

"My dad doesn't speak much French," Jules explained. "We speak English at home."

Jules opened his math book.

"Wow," Taylor said. "Cool."

Jules chuckled. Maybe today might be salvaged. When that last class dismissed, Jules raced to his locker (to get there before Benji). When Benji arrived, Jules had his Walkman in hand and slung his backpack over one shoulder. His flannel shirt fell down his arm.

"I'm not coming home. You need to go for Minette," Jules stated.

"*Ca quoi ce bordel?*" his brother asked which translated into "What's going on in this whorehouse?"

"I'm helping a friend study," he said.

"What friends?" Benji replied. "You don't have friends."

Taylor wove between the other students.

"Taylor! Let me introduce you to my brother, Benji."

"You just spoke French to me," Taylor said. "Seriously? Here? Now?"

"Salut, Taylor, but I prefer Louis," Benji replied, in English, heavy emphasis on the S in the last syllable of Louis. "See you later, Jules."

Benji smacked the back of Jules' skull and walked confidently away.

"Why do you call him Benji if his name is Louis?" Taylor asked.

"His name is Louis-Benedict. After my dad, Benedict, and my mother's father, Louis," Jules explained, complete with the French pronunciation of 'Louis,' Lou-ee.

"So Louis is his middle name," Taylor deducted.

"Not really. His middle name is Gabriel."

"Is your name really Jules? Or is it Jean-Jules Pierre or something?" Taylor teased.

"Jules Michael. My parents used up the extra names on Benji. And come to think of it, the French ones."

Jules hooked his headphones over his head but left one ear free. He pressed the play button. The disc spun.

"What are you listening to?" Taylor said, leaning toward the headphones. "Nirvana?"

They merged with wave of teenagers cascading toward the doors.

"Hey, how far is the nearest beach?" Jules asked Taylor.

"About an hour."

"An hour?" Jules said. He sighed. "Is there a bus?"

"I don't know," Taylor replied.

"That explains why my grandparents never took me."

Once outside, everyone dispersed in different directions. Most of the kids walked, and some, like Benji, followed the path to the elementary school. A handful of kids took the bus. Some of the seniors had parking passes and drove to school. Taylor pointed toward the gaggle of students moving toward Washington Street. Jules followed. While they waited at the corner for the light to turn, a pack of cavemen paraded toward them led by Bobby Lincoln.

"Hey, Jewel!"

Jules ignored the bastardization of his name and stared at the traffic light. Bobby gave Jules a hearty push from behind, knocking him into Taylor and causing Taylor to stumble off the curb. Jules hooked his hand into Taylor's elbow and steadied him. The petty, pick-on-the-new-kid bullshit wore thin after a couple weeks. Jules rolled his eyes at Bobby. Jules' heart rate picked up and his body tingled with adrenaline. Bobby had a hundred pounds over Jules, but Jules had a height advantage. In France, being six-foot-two was annoying and a tad freakish, but now, it gave Jules an edge. Bobby waved his French workbook.

"I heard you're helping Taylor tonight," Bobby said. "You need to do something for me."

The whole school knew Bobby was technically on academic probation and wouldn't be playing in any more football games—the American kind—until he improved his grades. Bobby did something resembling a grunt.

"How about you fill in pages 27 to 36?" Bobby suggested.

Bobby thrust the workbook toward Jules. Jules seized the book before it hit his torso and flipped it back at Bobby, where it bounced off Bobby's arm. It landed on the sidewalk. Sucking in a deep breath, Jules stepped toward his attacker, his face looming over Bobby's, looking down at him and imagining him as a tiny insect begging to be crushed. Jules squared his shoulders, clenched his fists and angled his arms ready to strike.

"I don't think so, Bobby."

Bobby blinked. Even his entourage froze. The walk signal turned green but nobody went.

"Let's go, Taylor."

Jules stepped into the crosswalk. Taylor followed. The other teenagers slowly joined them until the cavemen cluster stood abandoned.

"I'll be waiting for you tomorrow," Bobby shouted.

Without glancing back, Jules flashed Bobby his middle finger.

"*Ta mére!*" Jules yelled.

"You know he's going to kill you," Taylor said at the end of the next block.

"Oh dear God, California is the last place on Earth I want to die!"

"What's so bad about California?" Taylor asked.

"Not like Biarritz. The beach is within walking distance. The water is as blue as the sky. The women go topless. You can grab a beer and just watch them…"

Taylor lived in a typical conglomeration of stucco and terra cotta ranch houses arranged in a semi-circular pattern. Weaving through these neighborhoods made Jules dizzy. When they arrived at Taylor's house, Taylor headed straight for the kitchen and tossed his backpack on a table under the window. He slipped past the island and opened the fridge. He grabbed a two liter of Mountain Dew and, with his free arm, withdrew two glasses from a nearby cupboard. He placed them on the table.

"I'll be right back."

Taylor disappeared into a narrow hall beside the refrigerator. A white cat emerged. It walked tentatively toward Jules, pausing and arching its back every few steps. Jules poured himself some soda. The cat darted behind the garbage can. Taylor returned. He threw a small yellow projectile toward Jules. Jules caught it, crackling plastic beneath his fingers. It was a Twinkie.

"My mom won't buy these so I keep them hidden in my room," Taylor explained. "Since it's your last night and all… I figured…"

"Thanks," Jules said.

He tore open the wrapper. Taylor retrieved his French book and notes. The two of them sat at the table where they started the worksheet. A car drove up to the house. The garage door opened, which Jules heard through the kitchen wall. But then he smelled something, something salty and floral. It intensified, and Jules recognized it as sweat and perfume. Taylor's mom entered the house through the side door. She had a bag of groceries in each arm.

Jules lost his breath, unsure what to make of the fact that he had smelled Taylor's mother before she entered the room. Taylor didn't seem to notice. And it wasn't like she smelled bad… While the boys did homework, she mixed various ingredients in a large ceramic bowl. Jules puzzled over her scent. How could he smell her? She peeled a purple onion and diced it. That stung his eyes from across the room. She cracked an egg, adding that, and squirted massive amounts of ketchup. Jules wrinkled his nose. She poured breadcrumbs into the bowl.

"Jules, you're staring at my mom," Taylor said.

"What is she cooking?"

"Meatloaf," he answered. "I told you."

"Does she wear perfume?" Jules asked.

"Not usually, but she loves this weird soap from that store in the mall."

Taylor's mother smashed the beef mix with her bare hands, kneading it like bread dough and shaping it into a loaf. She sprinkled the top with what smelled like *origan*. He sniffed again. The potency struck him as strongly as if he had stuck his nose in the bottle and Taylor's mother had the dehydrated flakes on the far side of the kitchen. He directed his attention to teaching Taylor verb stems.

"So, Jules, you're the French boy," Taylor's mom said. "How are you holding up?"

"Bobby Lincoln is going to beat him up tomorrow," Taylor interjected.

"Oh, my. Isn't Bobby the captain of the football team?"

"Yeah, the rest of us lay low around him, but Jules wouldn't take his shit."

"Taylor! Language!"

"Sorry, Mom," Taylor said.

"I can't lay low," Jules replied quietly. "I'm too tall."

By the time they finished their homework, Jules had to head home. Taylor's mother suggested that she drive him, but Jules needed the two mile walk. He so missed his daily treks to the beach. He never found peace here, never got to clear his head. The sky shifted toward purple as if someone had poured Beaujolais into a tinted glass bowl of navy blue. Only the glow of the ripe moon punctured the darkness. Its light filtered through the clouds, obscuring the stars but creating silver fog overhead.

Who the fuck did Bobby Lincoln think he was? Jules thought to himself.

He kicked a soda can. It arched into the air and hit a tree, ricocheting off the trunk. He picked it up and placed it in a nearby garbage can. His parents' cars sat side-by-side in the driveway of their rental. The living room light was on, and he could see through that room that his family had gathered in the kitchen. He opened the door.

"*Coucou*, everyone," Jules called.

Minette ran into the foyer to hug him. He threw his backpack on the couch. His father poked his head into the living room from the kitchen.

"Hello, Jules. Benji said you were tutoring someone in French."

"Dad, it's Louis," Benji yelled from the family room.

"Taylor," Jules said. "He's in my math class."

From the kitchen, his mother's cutting knife clinked.

"Jules, I had to cut my own carrots," his mother said.

"Sorry, Mom. I meant to get home earlier but irregular verb stems..."

Minette plopped onto the couch in the family room, next to Benji playing Super Mario World. She grabbed the other controller. She had grown up on the Super Mario Brothers games. Their father poured a glass of wine for himself and then one for their mother. He carried the bottle toward the dining room. Their mother scooped the carrots into her cupped hands allowing them to rain over a roaster chicken in a classic black Le Creuset *cocotte*. She pointed her chin toward their spice rack.

"Could you?" she asked.

With nothing more, Jules plucked the grinder full of *herbs de provence*. He twisted heartily and released the fragrant blend across the chicken. His mother placed the lid on the *cocotte*. Jules lifted it into the oven. His father returned. His mother washed her hands.

"So how was school?" his mother asked.

Her French accent had never sounded so thick before they moved here. After listening to people speak harsh English all day, Jules realized how foreign his mother sounded.

"Academically, fine," Jules answered. "It's easier than school at home. I mean, in France. Here, teachers humiliate you a lot less. But the kids… Well, Benji, what would you say?"

"There's some hot chicks. Laura Portersmith keeps looking at me."

"So you're all making friends," their mother replied.

"A girl named Sally in my class invited me to her birthday party," Minette said.

Ten-year-old Minette beat the final level as she answered their mother's question.

"Oh, Min! You did it again. She always wins!" Benji whined.

"You boys taught her those games," their father replied.

"And then there's Taylor," their mother said, smiling at Jules. "You kids amaze me, the ease with which you can make friends."

Their mother beamed. It spurred a heaviness in Jules' heart because of what had happened with Bobby Lincoln. He wanted to tell his mother that American high school sucked. He yearned to admit that he had to avoid the bully on a regular basis. But he couldn't. He walked to the cupboard.

"I'll set the table," Jules said as he carried a pile of dishes into the dining room.

He slammed the plates onto the table. The silverware clattered as he tossed it into place. He lit the tapers on either end of the table. As they waited for the chicken to cook, Jules played a few rounds of cards with his sister. They ate, a quiet meal for his normally boisterous family.

"May I be excused?" Jules asked, crossing his utensils and placing his napkin on his plate.

"Whose turn is it to clean up?" their father responded.

"Mine," Benji said.

"Then, yes," their father replied.

Jules bid his family goodnight. He used the bathroom and brushed his teeth, which turned out a tad complicated since Benji had hidden Jules' toothbrush in the linen closet. His evening preparations complete, Jules went to the basement where he and Benji each had a temporary bedroom. His parents had rented this house until they finished building their cabin in the mountains, not far from his father's parents. Thanks to a quick geography lesson from Taylor, Jules realized that their new house would be another thirty minutes from the beach. An hour and thirty minutes. He might never surf again. He laid in his bed, staring at the ceiling and imagining breaking waves.

Footfalls crossed the kitchen and dining room floors as the family cleared the table and loaded the dishwasher. Come on, Benji, Jules thought as he listened, I really need to talk to you. His brother's footsteps eventually approached the stairs, but veered instead to the family room. The theme music from Mario World commenced. Jules scowled. He turned out the light.

For breakfast his mother prepared hot chocolate and thick slices of bread smeared with butter. A collection of jellies littered the table. Their father left for work. Minette waited by the door as Mother gathered her purse and her keys. Jules stood in the kitchen, placing his cup and saucer in the sink when he smelled blood. He checked his hands. Mother came to him, lips squeezed together for a kiss on the cheek. The smell pounded against him. His stomach flipped. The smell of blood surrounded him, tightened against him and made it difficult to breathe.

"*Bonne journée*, Jules," she said.

"*Bonne journée, Maman. A tout à l'heure.*"

She and Minette departed. Jules rushed into the bathroom. He slid to his knees in front of the toilet, heaving. Nothing but spit came up. When he lifted his head from the bowl, he noticed a tampon wrapper in the garbage can. Benji appeared in the doorway.

"You okay, man?"

"I don't know," Jules replied. "Nerves I guess."

"Nerves? About what?"

"I pissed off Bobby Lincoln yesterday. And he wants to fight me after school."

"You?!?!?"

"Yeah. He told me to suck his dick and I told him off and then he told me to do his French homework and I threw his book at him," Jules' speech doubled in speed. "And ever since then I can smell everything and it's gross. Like I could smell Taylor's mom before she came in the room. An onion made me cry from twenty feet away and apparently Mom has her period."

"We should leave for school."

"That's it, Benji? Bobby Lincoln is going to kill me!"

"Good luck with that, baby brother."

"Shit," Jules said as he pulled himself to his feet. "Maybe I could stay home."

"Then he'll beat you up tomorrow."

Jules grabbed his backpack.

"I'm not really worried," Jules said as his brother led the way. "I bet he's all talk."

"He's a football player, Jules. Those guys take a hit on the field all the time. They're not afraid of a fight."

Jules paused at the end of the walkway. "You know what, Benji? Neither am I."

"I got your back," Benji said.

Jules smiled. "Thanks. I've never been in a fight before."

Benji chortled. "But you've pinned me to the floor a few times, almost broke my arm, and have kneed me in the balls more times than I'd like to admit."

There it loomed—the school, a bleak fortress in the middle of suburbia. Benji and Jules went to their locker. Once Jules stepped into homeroom, every class zipped by in fast forward. Every time he took his seat, someone asked Jules if it were true that he had thrown a book at Bobby Lincoln. Some kids' mouths dropped open in awe, others implied that Jules' IQ had dropped. Laura Portersmith with her buxom body came over in French class. She smelled tangy, like nothing Jules recognized.

"Not many kids in this school would stand up to Bobby Lincoln," she said.

Jules shrugged. He inhaled, attempting to memorize her smell. At this distance, all he could discern was the sweetness of her bubble gum. The other scent, whatever it was, lay underneath.

"Well, if you can still walk when it's over, give me a call."

She took Benji's blue pen, turned over Jules' hand and wrote her phone number on his palm. She stood so close to him, but he still couldn't decipher the smell. She pulled away. Benji's face screwed into strange knots. Bobby might not be the only one wishing him ill today. Laura went to her desk.

"Give me my damn pen," Benji hissed in French.

Jules dropped the pen and sat down. He shifted in his seat. Laura's flirtations had inspired a physical reaction. He had trouble keeping up with class. She was right there, a few seats away and he could still smell her. His "reaction" to Laura's display of interest shouldn't have surprised him. He buttoned his flannel shirt in case it didn't settle before the end of class. He opened his hand and read the numbers. He copied them into his notebook. The smell lingered in the air, not that anyone else seemed to notice it. Jules not only noticed it, but he couldn't even think about anything else.

"Michel Zed," the teacher called.

Jules peered up, reluctantly. She meant him. "Madame" had this annoying preference that everyone in class had to have a French name, and she suggested Jules use the French version of his middle name since his first name couldn't easily be Frenchified, in her opinion. Benji loved this because she called him Louis even if she didn't pronounce the S.

"Madame, I do not call myself Michel," Jules answered in proper French. "My name is Jules and while I am sorry this does not please you, it is the name my French mother gave me."

Laura Portersmith suppressed her laughter but did not hide how she watched him.

The teacher offered a strained half-smile. "Can you answer how Mr. Dupont traveled to Avignon to visit his niece?"

"According to the story, he took the train and it was a long journey," he answered in French. "But this whore of a book is so old, any dope knows that the TGV runs between Paris and Avignon in two hours and forty minutes."

Benji grew wide-eyed in the next row. The teacher flushed. The class murmured and everyone gawked at Jules.

"Monsieur, I will be calling your parents," the teacher said.

"If mother answers," Jules replied, "feel free to speak French."

The bell rang.

"'This whore of a book,'" Benji said as he tugged Jules by the elbow toward their locker. "What has gotten into you?"

"That woman and her awful American accent is making me nuts!" Jules hollered. "If she talks to Mom, Mom will totally back me up. That woman cannot speak French!"

He slammed his books into the locker and punched the door. Benji stepped away.

"Okay, then. I'll see you later."

Benji left. Jules adjusted his backpack and headed toward his last class before lunch, biology. The hallways thinned of students, but a persistent odor of garlic and dirty gym clothes followed Jules. A consistent pattern of footsteps indicated two people. Jules stopped. They also stopped. Jules spun around to face them. He didn't know them, but the football jerseys suggested they were emissaries of Bobby Lincoln.

"What the fuck do you want?" Jules barked.

The smaller one stepped closer.

"Bobby wanted to remind you that he's going to kick your ass. Out front. After school."

Jules closed the gap between them, so that the one who'd spoken had to lift his chin to look at Jules. You couldn't pass a pencil between their noses.

"Bobby isn't going to get near my ass," Jules replied.

He stomped on the kid's foot and gave him a two-handed shove so he stumbled into the other guy. Jules strode to biology and entered the classroom as the bell rang. A tremble went through his body and his muscles relaxed. He flexed his fingers, open and closed them to release more tension, and then he exhaled. The ever-present stain of formaldehyde over the room made his head ache. He rubbed it as the teacher drew a flow chart of a butterfly's life cycle. This day might never end.

But it did. Taylor was the first one at his locker, then Benji, and then some other guys who leaned against the wall on the other side of the hallway, all of them waiting for what might happen. The girls walked by, slowly, pretending to not care, but casting sideways glances toward him. Without saying anything to anyone, he headed toward the front of the school. Taylor and his brother each protectively flanked a side.

The metallic clang of locker doors, the flecks of dust in the sunlight dancing across the halls, the blank faces as the kids he passed, everything swirled into a funnel. Jules thought only of Bobby Lincoln. He stepped outside, the bright sun blinding him as he traced his adversary by nose to the edge of school property. Jules dropped his backpack into the grass.

Bobby Lincoln stood with his back to the sidewalk, his hands on his hips and a constipated expression on his meathead face. Jules marched to him, extended his index finger, and with all his force poked the soft spot at the bottom of Bobby's neck between his collarbones. Bobby's head dove forward as he gagged. As Bobby folded, Jules delivered a solid left hook to his jaw. That, of course, bounced Bobby's head upward so Jules walloped him with a right-handed punch square against Bobby's nose. His nostrils spewed blood into the grass, puddles of red from a human spigot. The coppery aroma spurred Jules onward as adrenaline surged.

A circle had gathered around them. To Jules, it was a ring of shadows hiding him and his prey from the authorities. Jules shook out his hands and flashed a wicked smirk. Bobby's white face progressed to glowing magenta as the boy touched his nose. Bobby scrunched his face, grunted, and leapt toward Jules, seizing Jules with both hands around the neck. Jules snapped his knee into Bobby's nuts. Bobby curled into himself and fell. Jules waited. The crowd gasped and muttered in shock that Bobby had gone down.

"The French kid won't take your shit, Bobby," Jules said.

He leaned toward his backpack. Bobby clamored to his feet, blood caking one side of his face as he stood cock-eyed. His eyes had already hinted at the bruising that would appear later. Jules reached for his bag's strap when Bobby swung. He hit Jules where his jaw, ear and neck met. Jules threw the backpack.

"Really, bitch?" Jules said, opening his arms and facing Bobby. "You want more?"

The crowd roared. Bobby took another pathetic hit at Jules, a punch to the chest that felt like Minette had thrown it. Something rippled toward Jules. Benji looked anxiously toward the school and then to Jules. Jules inhaled through his nose sensing Laura Portersmith. Her smell had intensified, salty and earthy. He sought her face, met her eyes and finally solved the puzzle.

Arousal. Laura Portersmith smelled like sex.

Filing that scent away, Jules studied the air for other familiar signatures. He smelled the principal and the French teacher. This fight wouldn't last much longer. Bobby, apparently energized by Jules' lack of reaction to the previous blows, landed another hit to Jules' jaw. Jules inhaled again, the smells of blood, sex, and human emotion triggering more adrenaline that burned into his muscles. He pounded Bobby with rapid blows reducing Bobby's face to a purple, blood-stained gob. Jules smashed him to the ground as the crowd stopped cheering.

The smells changed as he pummeled Bobby. They blended urine, sweat, and blood into a light sweetness topped with fear. Bobby could only open one eye. He stopped returning blows. Jules gripped Bobby's shirt as his legs straddled Bobby. Jules released him as the principal wove through the crowd and the French teacher screamed in French for Jules to stop as if that language would saturate his brain quicker than English.

At least she didn't call him "Michel Zed" this time. Jules laughed.

The principal grabbed Jules by the collar. "It's not funny, Zweigenbaum."

Bobby rolled on the ground, crying.

"So much for the goddamned underdog," Benji yelled in French.

Jules shook out his hand and wiped the blood on his shirt, except what he thought was blood didn't come off. He swiped the hand across the fabric again. Still unable to remove it, Jules examined his hand in the sunlight. It wasn't blood on his fingers, but thick black hair that had appeared on his knuckles.

"Get him to the nurse," the principal said pointing at Bobby.

Bobby's posse of football players stood shell-shocked and slack-jawed.

"Zweigenbaum, to my office," the principal commanded.

Jules lifted his backpack from the ground and the crowd surrounding him parted as he stepped toward the school. He stopped in front of Laura.

"I'm still standing," Jules said.

"Later, Zweigenbaum. To my office," the principal repeated.

"I'll call you," Jules told Laura.

Her heart raced, and her smell had not changed. Jules went toward the building. The principal yammered at everyone to go home, except for Benji. The principal made Benji sit in the hall. Jules went to the darkest corner behind the principal's desk. The principal closed the door.

"I haven't heard a peep from you since you arrived at this school," the principal said. "Now what the hell was that?"

Jules chuckled. The principal had an elevated heart rate and a tremor to his hands. The smell of fear stretched between them. Jules' back itched. He stood against the wall to scratch it. Then his belly itched. He pulled one hand free and stuck it under his shirt. His fingers sunk into a swatch of fur, even thicker than the hair on his knuckles. He withdrew his hand and shoved it into his pocket.

"Every kid in this school would love to hit Bobby Lincoln," he answered.

"And you, the new kid, decided to let him have it."

Jules shrugged. He walked to the principal and met the man's eyes. He looked so deep into the man's face that the principal's shaking increased. The normal Jules wouldn't have noticed, but this heightened senses, high-on-adrenaline Jules noticed everything.

"What are you going to do about it?" Jules asked.

"I'm calling your parents. You're suspended for three days."

Jules went into the hall. Benji was not there.

"Where's my brother?" he asked the secretary.

"Your mom came," she said.

"And she didn't wait for me?"

"She said you were to wait for your father."

Jules plopped into a nearby chair. "Dad? Really?"

The secretary nodded. When his father arrived, Jules met him at his red Mazda RX7 convertible. The top was down. Jules tossed his school bag on the floor. His father opened a small leather satchel.

"Jules," his father said as he pulled a piece of blue litmus paper from a tube, "I'm going to ask you some questions. I need you to be honest."

He handed Jules the strip.

"Set that on your tongue please," his father directed.

"Dad? It's litmus paper."

"I know what it is, Jules. Do it."

Jules obeyed. It tasted like salty chemicals. His father retrieved a rubber strap from the bag. He took Jules' arm and tied the strap in a bow. Jules removed the litmus paper and showed the now pink strip to his father.

"Dad? Why are you…"

His father removed a needle and a plastic vial from the bag. He put on disposable gloves.

"Dad!"

His father took Jules' arm, turning the white inside of Jules' elbow toward him.

"Dad! *Ce quoi ce bordelle?* Are you drawing my blood?"

The needle pierced the vein.

"Dad!"

His father filled the vial, untied the strap, labeled the vial, and placed it in the bag. He then took the litmus paper.

"All this time I suspected Benji," his father said, waving the now mostly pink litmus paper. "Okay, so Jules, have you recently engaged in sexual activity?"

"What?!? Dad! What is going on? I got in a fight. Aren't you supposed to ground me? I mean, you have hardly said two words to me. You made me lick litmus paper, took my blood and want to know if I'm having sex? Dad! I got in a fight. I haven't come down with a sexually transmitted disease."

"Are you?"

"You're serious?" Jules replied. He sighed. "Fuck, no."

"Are you a virgin?" his father asked.

Jules looked to his father, whose expression had not budged from the stony serious face he had since arriving.

"Yes, Dad. Happy now?"

His father's eyebrows wavered. He pinched his lips with the gloved hand not holding the litmus paper.

"This doesn't make any sense," his father said.

"Imagine how I feel," Jules responded.

"Are you sure?" his father asked. He dropped the litmus paper into his bag.

"Yeah," Jules confirmed. "That's not something you can be uncertain about."

"I need to talk to your mother," his father said, peeling off the gloves and starting the car.

"Can you talk to me, Dad? You're acting really weird. Aren't you supposed to ask why I beat the shit out of him?"

His father pulled out onto the road.

"Let's talk," his father said. "You're not sexually active. The PH in your mouth is highly acidic. You are showing an unusual spike of aggression coinciding with the full moon. Any other symptomatic behavior you want to let me know about?"

"Like symptoms of a disease? I can smell stuff."

"Like phantom smells?"

"No, smells that are there. Just no one else smells them. Like distinguishing people by smell. From a distance. And I could smell that Mom has her period."

"Anything else?"

"It started after the fight," Jules said. He displayed his black hairy knuckles. "What do I have, Dad? I have something right? A disease? An abnormality?"

"Did you ever ask yourself why I've spent my life researching genetics, wound healing, hormones and neurotransmitters?" his father asked.

"Because you're a geek?" Jules answered.

They had reached home.

"I have to run some tests, but this…" his father said, waving the discarded litmus paper, "…is fairly conclusive evidence that you have inherited a genetic condition that usually activates upon sexual maturity, but it would make sense that emotional stress can trigger early onset…"

"So, you think I'm sick?" Jules interrupted. "I'm an overly testosteroned schizophrenic?"

His father raised the roof on the car.

"No, Jules. You're a werewolf."

His father stepped out of the car.

"Uh, Dad?" Jules replied, chasing after him. "There's no such thing."

"Ready for some family secrets, Jules? My father was a werewolf. Your mother's great-great-something grandfather was a werewolf," his father said. "It's a recessive trait requiring heterogametic sex chromosomes that both carry extra DNA. Wolf DNA."

They entered the house.

"That's fucked up, Dad."

"Watch your language, Jules."

With her arm around Minette, his mother darted from the kitchen into the family room.

"Benji, take your sister to your room," she ordered in French.

"To my room? Why can't she go to her own room?" Benji asked.

"Because your room is—"

"Margot!" his father interrupted. "They should be here for this."

His mother threw up her arms.

"To the table. Everyone. Family meeting," his father said.

Mother reversed course into the dining room, Minette and Benji on her heels. Father followed. Jules meandered through the living room. He attributed this whole day to a bad dream produced by the stress of the anticipation of whatever Bobby Lincoln might do to him. Tomorrow. Because none of this could be happening.

Jules finally reached the dining room table, his father stood at the head with his mother and his older brother on either side. Minette sat beside their mother so Jules slouched into the chair near Benji.

"First, I'm sorry I haven't told you this before," their father began, "but our family carries a genetic abnormality of dual DNA. In most cases, the extra DNA lays dormant. Jules has inherited this condition."

His siblings had the same blank, confused expression Jules must have had.

"Wait!" Jules yelled, slapping the table. His siblings jumped. "Not only do you expect me to believe this, but you and Mom knew you carried a recessive trait that you could pass on?"

Jules loomed over the table, hovering over his brother toward his father. His mother whimpered.

"We didn't know anything," his father said in an elevated voice. "Genetic testing didn't exist until after all of you were born. It has taken most of my career to put the smallest clues of this puzzle together. So I'm sorry I couldn't work fast enough to prevent this."

His mother reached for Jules' hand.

"We had no proof in my family. There are legends, a couple hundred years old," she said.

"Yo!" Benji called. "Would someone mind filling me in? I never got the memo. What is this hereditary ailment? Do I have it?"

"Ready for this, Benj," Jules said, backing away from the table. "Instead of asking why I beat up Bobby Lincoln at school today, Dad, and apparently Mom, think I'm a werewolf."

Benji scoffed. Jules stepped into the hallway. He faced his family.

"Why is it so hard to believe that maybe," Jules screamed and waved his arms for emphasis, "I simply got tired of the shit Bobby's dealt for the last three weeks."

"Calm down, Jules," his mother responded. "That won't help."

Benji laughed.

"It's not a joke, Benji," their father said.

"I'm not a werewolf! Maybe I grew some balls," Jules yelled.

He stomped from the room. Something clattered. Something else rustled. His mother yelped. His sister screamed. A chair fell backward onto the floor. Jules doubled back to the dining room. His father gripped his mother's neck inside his elbow as her hands tugged on his arm. With his other hand, he held a gun against Mother's head. Minette had dropped under the table, hugging her knees to her chest as tears stained her cheeks. Benji flattened himself against the wall. Multiple waves of fear washed across the room.

In a fraction of a second, Jules leapt to the dining room table, raced across it and knocked his father into the sliding glass door behind him and to the floor. Jules then shifted his weight to the table and stood there, still watching Father. Jules' mother rolled away. The gun dropped. Benji retrieved it and aimed it at their father who was rubbing his head.

"Holy shit," Benji said.

Benji swung the gun toward Jules, away from their father. Their mother approached.

"Everyone, stay calm," she said. "I have asked from the beginning that everyone stay calm. But no one listens. None of you listen to me."

Father got to his feet. He extended a hand to Benji. "Give me the gun."

"I don't think so, Dad," Benji said. Jules could feel his brother shaking. "You pulled a gun on Mom, and then Jules… Jules…"

Their mother hid her face behind her hands and cried.

"Turned into a wolf," their father said.

Minette scrambled from her hiding place and reappeared near her seat.

"Whoa," she said.

She stretched her hand toward Jules. Their mother slapped her fingers. Jules growled and postured toward their mother.

"Don't touch him!" Mother snapped.

Their father crept toward Benji. "Now, Margot, everything is under control."

"Under control!" she half-screamed as she wept. "There's a gun in my dining room and we're threatening to shoot each other."

"Margot, you know it's a tranquilizer gun," their father said. He offered an open palm to Benji. "I only threatened your mother to help Jules understand."

"Next time, chose a safer plan," Margot retorted.

Benji handed their father the gun. Jules and his father stared at each other, the only sounds in the room their mother's stifled crying and an occasional clock tick. Darkness had fallen outside. In the black mirror of the sliding glass door, Jules saw his reflection as a wolf. He laid down on the table and hid his eyes with his paws.

"Am I a werewolf?" Benji asked, uncertainty in his voice.

"Am I?" Minette also asked, her voice exuberant and excited.

"I don't know, Benji," their father replied.

"No, Minette," their mother said. "Girls can't be werewolves."

"No fair!" she said, planting her hands on her hips as she marched into the hallway. After about ten footsteps, her bedroom door slammed.

Jules hopped off the table.

"Jules," his father called, "where are you going?"

A canine whimper emerged from his mouth. To my room, he wanted to say. Instead, he trotted into the hall and down the stairs. His father followed. Jules leapt onto his bed. His father set a bottle of pills on Jules' desk.

"It's treatable," his father said.

After his father ground some pills and mixed the dust into applesauce, Jules lapped up the concoction and went to sleep. He woke late the next morning, naked, curled in a fetal position on his blankets. He threw on some sweatpants and a t-shirt before going upstairs. His dad slept in the recliner closest to the stairwell, the tranquilizer gun in his hand. Jules brushed his arm.

"Dad?"

His father jerked awake, awkwardly waving the tranquilizer gun.

"Easy there, Dad."

His father dropped the gun and got out of his seat, moving slowly toward the kitchen. He made them some scrambled eggs, diced potatoes and lamb sausage while they discussed what had happened. Apparently Jules had to take medication, primarily a benzodiazepine with an extremely low dose of an anti-psychotic. If Jules didn't, the flood of adrenaline and testosterone that could result would prompt the wolf DNA to hijack his body. The approach of the moon would increase his body's normal level of hormones, also amplifying his newly-discovered aggression, which could also lure the wolf out of him. His father also had a warning.

"You probably shifted because of the psychological stress of moving," he said, "but normally, it's the first sexual encounter that provides enough endorphins and hormones to prompt the change. That's when subjects report the increase in aggression, the other symptoms."

"So what happens if I have sex?"

"Well, Jules, I'm not sure."

"You've studied werewolves your whole life!" Jules replied.

"You're the fifth one I've seen. It's not like there are hundreds. You haven't turned into a werewolf, you went straight to wolf form."

"So if I have sex, I might change into something else?"

"Maybe," his father said. "A werewolf is a form that's primarily human, but has wolf traits… Some strengths, some weakness. The werewolf is instinctual. You won't control it."

"Oh, that's reassuring. If I have sex, I'll turn into a monster," Jules said.

His brother brought home daily reports from school. Jules had broken Bobby Lincoln's nose but no other significant damage, "other than making his already ugly face purple and swollen," Benji said. Taylor called, as did Laura. She offered to stop by after school to drop off any books or homework he needed. To distract himself, Jules jogged. He'd rather be surfing but his family promptly vetoed the idea. One by one the other teenagers trickled from their houses and talked to him. When he returned to school, he had a crowd horning into his lunch table. Bobby Lincoln walked by with tape over his nose.

"Hey, Bobby," Jules yelled from across the lunch room, "maybe when you're feeling better you can help me write my English paper."

Everyone burst into laughter.

"Fuck you, Zweigenbaum!"

"That's the succinctness I need to emulate," Jules said. "French people tend to be wordy."

Before long a full week had passed since the fight, and Bobby Lincoln looked almost like his normal self again. Jules arrived in the gym for his PE class. Coach Klide had soccer balls on the sidelines. Jules smiled. The class divided into teams. Jules dashed across the gym floor and made four goals. His team won the game 5-0. Coach Klide recruited him for the varsity soccer team which had barely scored in three years. Laura squealed and kissed him when she heard the news. Benji joined the team, too, as goaltender.

The opponents underestimated them on the field, expecting the same team they'd faced in previous matches. Jules swept across the grass with precision and speed, his teammates focused on keeping his path free. When someone stole the ball, Jules sailed in front of them, attacking the ball with a fearlessness that often ended with a tangle of legs and complaints of kicked shins. With Benji guarding the net, any ball salvaged would be kicked out seamlessly to Jules. While their teamwork and prowess on the field meant unprecedented wins, depending on the moon phase, Jules racked up as many yellow and red cards as he did points. They won regionals, with the help of a waxing moon, and earned a spot in the state championship. Coach Klide gave Jules a stern lecture about his "temper," since he didn't want his star player ejected from the big game. Benji packed their gear. Mom and Minette were waiting outside the locker room.

"What happens if you go off your meds?" Benji asked.

"Why would I do that?" Jules said. "I get in enough trouble with them."

"You're a machine when the moon is full. If the championship is next month, I'm thinking it would give us an edge."

"That's cheating," Jules said.

"No way!" his brother replied, wrapping his arm around Jules. "The drugs hold you back. It's not like you're taking steroids. I'm suggesting embracing the all-natural Jules."

They headed for the door.

"I don't know, Benji. I could hurt someone."

"Maybe there's a better way," he said.

Jules exhaled in exasperation. Benji leaned in closer to his brother's ear.

"Start fucking Laura," Benji suggested.

Jules shook his brother's arm free of his shoulder. "This is such a joke to you, isn't it?"

He stormed from the locker room. Minette jumped vigorously. His mother clapped. Jules didn't even look at their faces.

"I'm walking home," he growled.

"I was thinking we'd go out to eat," his mother suggested.

"The food sucks around here," Jules remarked.

He accelerated his pace and pounded through the front door to find Laura, illegally parked in the fire zone and sitting on the hood of her Chevy Cavalier with a ski rack. She wore her cheering uniform, the short pleated skirt revealing endless leg from her upper thigh to her cute little ankle socks. She twirled her long blond hair around her finger.

"Hey," she said, sliding off the car. "That was an awesome game. Too bad we don't cheer for soccer."

She wrapped her arms around his neck and brushed her mouth against his, parting his lips with her tongue. Her warmth, scent and touch dissolved his anger, replacing it with a thousand dancing flames surging toward her. His arms enveloped her. His mouth pressed against hers. His hand followed her leg under her skirt. Laura pulled free.

"You want a ride home?" she asked.

Yes. Yes. Yes. Yes. Yes. Yes. Yes. The air around him hung thick with hormones. His clothes burned his body with every breath. She pointed to the car as his mother and siblings exited the school. His mother paused. Benji and Minette walked toward the car.

"I don't think that's a good idea," he said.

But he couldn't move. His body hurt too much.

"Jules?" his mother called. "*Vas-y.*"

"I should go," he said. "I need to get cleaned up."

Laura shrugged. "Okay. But call me."

She got into her car. As she drove away, his mother waited.

"Are you coming with us?" she asked.

"I need space, *Maman*," he replied.

"I want you home before dark," she said.

"*Ouias, maman.*"

She got into the car with his siblings and he started toward home. He really ached to surf, and if they hadn't left France he would have walked to the beach. If he stood very still, and inhaled very deeply, he could almost smell the Pacific. He broke into a run. It was a jog at first, but it escalated to a run when he thought about his coach, Benji, his mother, Laura. He clocked a four-and-a-half minute mile on his self-imposed race to the house. He showered, called Laura and, against his better judgment, invited her over. Laura went straight to the refrigerator and retrieved a big bowl of purple grapes.

"We need to talk," she said. She held the bowl in front of her. "I thought you'd be different, being French and all, but you're like oblivious or something."

She set the bowl on the counter and kissed him, the kind of kiss that made his toes tremble. The sweetness of grapes surrounded them. She pushed one between his lips.

"We're alone," she observed.

He chewed the grape. "Yeah, but, that's not why I asked you to come."

"It's not?" she said as she popped a grape into her mouth.

"I don't know why I asked you here."

"You don't?"

Her breath brushed across his face. She pushed her body into his until they fell against the counter. His knuckles itched. He rubbed them against his jeans to scratch them. She lifted the grapes between their faces. She bit one. He bit some. His taste buds exploded with the vibrancy of the fruit. Laura trotted backwards, luring him with the grapes. He chased after them. He latched onto the grapes, simultaneously seizing her waist and slamming their bodies together. Jules' hands itched, so did his stomach, but the rest of his body urged him forward, eating the grapes and finding her lips on the other side of the fruit. They rolled across the linoleum. She slipped her hands inside the back of his jeans and sunk her fingers into the cushion of his ass.

He couldn't let her go. He certainly couldn't move his lips from hers. He redirected his hands toward his fly fumbling with the button, distracted by her kiss, even more sidetracked by the level of uncomfortableness in his pants. He finally unbuttoned, unzipped, and as he welcomed a new sense of freedom, a pain from inside his skull forced his vision purplish-black. At the same time, Laura's mouth totally consumed his, her tongue probing and penetrating. His jaw shifted, his teeth moved, and something burst from his gums as he dropped to the floor.

Laura screamed. He had trouble balancing, even on all fours. The pain coursed through his entire skull, leaving him unable to open his eyes, unable to do anything but lean his face against the cool linoleum. Laura ran her hand along his back, her flesh so icy he had to be feverish. She kept screaming, and the pitch punctured his eardrums. He couldn't hear anything over her. A violent seizure consumed his whole body as his hands erupted in fur. Jules inched his head from the floor. He opened one eye and tried to scan the room. Where had he left his backpack? On the table… So far away… He slithered toward it, still shaking, his bones exploding. Dark colors surrounded Laura, who screamed more. Jules threw his arm toward the table and collapsed, unable to fight the convulsions as something jammed his nose.

Jules wanted to tell her he needed his backpack, that he needed the medicine inside, but the words came out as a howling whine. Laura was running around the kitchen, still screaming. Jules let the cold from the floor sink into his forehead. His fingernails lengthened and curled. He folded his hands into fists to hide them.

Please don't change, he thought to himself. Please.

His legs flailed. He thought he heard his mother's car. He couldn't be sure because of Laura's infernal noise. His jaw shifted forward. His chin stretched. He kept his face to the floor so should Laura calm down she wouldn't see him. The door squeaked. Laura sobbed. His mother's scent filled the room.

"*Ce quoi ce bordelle?*" she asked.

Minette and Benji scurried across the room.

"Get his pills!" Benji shouted as he dropped to his knees besides Jules. Benji pulled Jules to his side. That made it harder to control his limbs and fight the convulsions. "Oh Hell!"

Minette tossed the medication bottle to Benji who popped the cap and shook the pills into Jules' mouth. Jules swallowed a few, a bunch landed in his cheek and he let them dissolve there. He tucked his knees to his chest.

"Just a minute," Benji whispered so only Jules could hear. Benji pushed Jules' legs away enough so he could refasten Jules' pants.

In the living room, Jules' mother settled Laura onto the sofa and rushed into the kitchen with everyone else. The shaking had stopped, but Jules' face throbbed and he couldn't budge from the kitchen floor. His mother got on the floor beside him and lifted his head into her lap. She pushed his hair out of his face and stroked his forehead.

"My poor darling," she said in French. "I never should have left you."

"Mrs. Zweigenbaum?" Laura said from the arch between the living room and the kitchen. "Is he alright?"

"Yes, *chérie*, he is fine. Why don't you go home?"

"We were eating grapes and he had this horrible seizure…"

"It must have been the excitement from the game," his mother said. "Please, go home."

Laura came farther into the kitchen and Benji intercepted her.

"He's okay," Benji said. "Minette, walk Laura to the door."

"Jules?" Laura said. "I just want to say goodbye."

Jules grew drowsy.

"You will talk to him in school," his mother said. "But perhaps not tomorrow."

Footsteps headed into the living room. The door opened and closed. His brother returned to the kitchen. His mother pulled away from Jules and stood. Each moment took longer than the previous. A fog descended and he no longer saw his family, only felt and heard them.

"Can you take him to his room?" his mother asked Benji.

Benji came closer. He held Jules by the shoulders and tugged him. Jules did not move.

"No," Benji replied.

The eerie quietness of uneasy sleep followed. When he woke, he found himself drowning in Minette's scent. He opened his eyes to Minette's pink striped pillowcase, his body covered by a My Little Pony sleeping bag. He threw it off and peeled himself off the kitchen floor. His body ached and his head still throbbed. With the blanket in hand, he stumbled toward the stairs.

His father slept in the chair, in the same position as last time but without the tranquilizer gun. Jules ran into the wall. His father leapt from his seat.

"Jules!"

"Hey, Dad. Really, I don't think the stakeout is necessary. I'm not going to hurt anybody."

"Actually," his father said quietly as he reached to the end table. "I have this for you."

His father held up a needle.

"What is it?" Jules asked.

"You've got to be in a lot of pain. It's morphine."

"Morphine!"

"Let me help you," his father hooked his arm under Jules'.

They went downstairs and into Jules' room. Jules collapsed on his bed, holding his head and fighting tears. His father injected him with the morphine.

"Sleep well, Jules."

The weight of his body against his bed lightened. His bedroom walls faded away, and his blankets carried him into the night sky like a flying carpet. His muscles relaxed and the pain melted from him, dripping from the blankets and forming new stars. His blankets climbed toward the glowing moon, still full and gleaming white, the stars dancing amid its light. The stars circled something, something he could not see. In the glimpses between the stars as they danced, he thought he saw an animal shape in sparkling silver.

"Welcome, Jules," a woman's voice said. "We have great plans for you."

"You do?" he said. The voice gave him *deja vû*.

The vague animal/woman motioned to the stars, who immediately stopped dancing and let her cross their circle. She approached Jules, who recognized her as a wolf of blinding platinum whose size matched the moon herself. Jules gazed toward the moon and realized that she had gone, or had she?

"They call me Luna," she told him.

She placed her chilled, rubbery nose against his forehead as if to kiss him. The sun stretched its limbs over the horizon.

"I must go," she said.

Luna transformed from the wolf into the round moon. The sun rose and Luna descended. Jules squinted from the brightness of the sun, streaming into the window of his room. His brother carried a tray of croissants and coffee to his bed.

"So, what happened?" Benji asked as he sat beside Jules.

"I met the moon," he muttered.

"Is that a werewolf euphemism?" Benji asked.

Jules rubbed his face.

"Last night?" Jules said. "I guess it's like *Maman* said, the excitement of the game."

"Nice try," Benji replied. "I found you and I fixed your pants. You're welcome."

"Nothing happened," he said.

"Something happened," Benji said. "Did she do something?"

"No," Jules replied. "She didn't have a chance."

"I thought maybe—"

"No, Benji. No chance of me getting laid anytime this century," he remarked. "What did I look like? Oh my God! Laura!"

"Laura was too hysterical to see anything. Your fingers were like claws, and your nose was really wide and long and you had pointy teeth," Benji said. "And Dad says he's going to take you for an MRI. He's called four hospitals already. He took your meds and told Mom that he wants to give you injections instead so he could record your reactions on the MRI."

Jules pushed the tray to Benji and jumped from bed, fighting the wooziness as his feet awkwardly hit the floor. Leaving breakfast on the bed, Benji steadied him.

"What are you doing?" Benji asked.

"Leaving," Jules replied. "There's no way I'm letting Dad poke me like some lab rat and lay me out in a machine. It's not happening."

"Where will you go?" Benji said.

"The beach," he answered.

"Oh, yeah, Mom and Dad would never look for you at the beach," Benji retorted. "How will you get there? It's fifty miles away."

"Laura has a car."

"And she's going to help you after last night?"

"Maybe. If you ask her. And come with us."

"Oh yeah, so we'll all end up grounded for life."

"You can come home before the end of the school day," Jules pointed out.

"And let you have all the good surf? No way."

"Then find Laura."

Jules went to his bureau and fished out his boardshorts. He moved next toward the closet, throwing the shorts on the bed. He pulled his wet suit from its hanger.

"Now pack these in your gym bag, and I'll grab some food and wine. We just need to work around Dad."

"How are we going to get our boards out of the garage?" Benji asked.

"Get Laura. Take our suits. I'll get our boards. Meet me at the end of the block."

"Benji!" their father called down the stairs. "You're going to be late for school!"

"What about me, Dad?" Jules yelled.

"You aren't going to school," their father replied.

"But, Dad, I'm fine," Jules said. "I have to go to school."

"Not until I examine you," their father said.

Jules leaned into Benji, *"Bonne chance, mon frère."*

Benji rushed to his room, presumably to repack his gym bag.

"Benji!" their father called again.

Jules threw on his boots. He climbed the stairs. Benji followed.

"Do I really have to stay home?" Jules asked.

Benji left, so only their father and Jules remained in the house. Jules poured himself a glass of milk, masking his survey of the contents of the refrigerator. It'd be easy to score a bottle of wine, but he wasn't sure if they had readily accessible food stuffs. He noted a wheel of Camembert, plenty of fruit, and a bag of baby carrots. He closed the refrigerator and set his glass on the counter. He wished he had a normal American family, one that had blueberry muffins hanging around, but he didn't.

"I need to take you in for some important tests," his father said, "but I'm having trouble finding a lab with open equipment."

"What do we need tests for?" Jules asked.

"I want to study your brain, and how it reacts to stress. And your bone structure. I've never met a werewolf who hasn't engaged in sexual relations—"

"Dad! I know this is what you do," Jules interrupted, "but I'm not a test subject."

"Jules, I don't think you understand the severity of your condition—"

"I understand, Dad! Maybe you need to understand that you don't own me." Jules stomped from the kitchen. "I'm going to take a shower. And I need to shave."

"Fine," his father said. "I'll be in the living room making phone calls."

Once in the bathroom, Jules propped himself against the door and tried to think. If his father was in the living room, Jules couldn't get out the front door. The other easy way out was the sliding glass door in the dining room. Could he get through the kitchen unnoticed? Jules started the shower. He crept out of the bathroom and tiptoed down the hall. He peeked around the corner. His father was on the phone, staring out the front window. Jules slipped through the kitchen. Into the dining room he went, grabbing a bottle of red wine from the buffet, sliding open the door and running across the patio. He went around front to the garage and opened the garage bay carefully. He lifted his board off the wall, then Benji's. Their surf bag was on the floor. He placed the wine inside. He hoped Benji had money. Jules stuffed some rope inside the bag, too, before slinging it onto his shoulder. He tucked his board under his right arm and finagled Benji's under his left and broke into a run, straight toward the designated meeting spot. He didn't know what he'd do if his brother wasn't there.

But he was. And Laura was. They tied the boards to Laura's ski racks. Luckily, Benji had some towels stuffed in his repacked gym bag that could help cushion them.

"It's not even sixty degrees outside," Laura said, "and you're going into the ocean?"

"This is when the surfing starts," Jules said. "You've lived in California your whole life and you don't know this?"

"I don't surf."

Benji stuck his head out the car window from the backseat. "We'll teach you."

As soon as Benji said it, Jules' stomach turned in knots. He didn't want to teach Laura to surf. Surfing was his time, and he didn't want to waste it on someone else. Learning a new surf spot would demand enough of his attention. He had no desire to make this about Laura. The ride to the beach went quickly enough. They cruised the surf shops and chatted up the local surfers. In Biarritz, they had their spot. Jules and Benji knew the culture, but here… This meant starting over. Newcomers had to respect the local ways.

They made their way to the beach, claimed their corner of the sand and got ready to surf. Laura screeched in protest as Jules and Benji stripped to put on their boardshorts, but even though she covered her eyes at their nudity, he could see her open eyes behind her fingers. Wet suits zipped, boards waxed, leashes on. Jules jogged closer to the shore, staring at the waves as they rolled and broke. It had been too long. Benji claimed his birthright as the older sibling and paddled into the water first. Jules followed, but gave Benji a wide berth and didn't even try to catch anything. The swell, with waves at about 1.5 meters, would push Benji to the shore from the northwest. And so Jules waited, floating with his board, paddling toward some small waves to practice a few turtle rolls.

He rolled to the top of his board in time to see Benji pop up. Benji wavered but kept his balance, riding the wave to the shore. That meant his turn. Jules paddled out, past the first few waves, to where the water grew deeper and the chance of a good barrel increased. These were new waters, but they felt familiar. The rhythm felt right as he turned his board around and this time paddled toward shore as quickly as he could. He should watch the wave over his shoulder but he could feel its approach, hear its demands. The wave carried him upward. He popped to his feet, and then he waited, listened, balanced. He leaned into the wave at just the right moment, slid his hand into it, and backed into the barrel.

And from there, he rocked it. He sped across the wave and, keeping his eye on the window, savored every second of dancing on air. The water crashed around him. A rich green surrounded him. When he flew out, he mounted the white water and rode it up and down to the shore, zigzagging as if he'd never let that wave go. His brother's jaw hung open.

"You've never surfed like that," Benji said. "And these are new waters!"

Jules shrugged. "Luck?"

"Jules, that was amazing," Benji insisted.

He shrugged again. "I listened to the water."

"Do you think…your condition had anything to do with it?"

"Can't I be good at something?" Jules asked.

Jules carried his board away from the ocean and pierced the sand with the tip. He dropped onto the beach, pulling his knees to his chest and staring toward the horizon. Benji swam out and took another wave. His body moved fluidly with the board and the wave. Closing his eyes, Jules' body relaxed imagining riding it himself. The warmth cleansed his nostrils.

Eyes still closed, Jules sensed someone nearby. His nose confirmed it was Laura. Her shadow blocked his sunlight, and suddenly, she had plopped into the sand beside him. He opened his eyes, facing her. She smiled. Without a word, she reached to his knees, where he had clasped his hands. She laid her fingers over his.

In the distance, Jules could see the moon. The clouds rolled across the sweet blue of the sky, the scent of salt filled his sinuses, and despite the brightness of the California sun, Jules stared at the moon. And he wondered about his future. Would he still be the quiet French kid—or would the wolf forever taint his life?

ABOUT THE AUTHOR

THE BEAUTY OF WORDS has infiltrated the life of Angel Ackerman for her entire life — from reading *Green Eggs and Ham* thousands of times to writing groundbreaking poems titled "My mom wears flip-flops" in Mrs. Sanders' second-grade class. She started the *Fashion and Fiends* series at the age of 16 and rewrote the novel *Manipulations* at least ten times before declaring this version "the one" in 2016.

Angel spent 15 years as a print journalist, specializing in weekly newspapers where reporters learned to write about every topic and take their own photographs. With the decline of print media, Angel explored the non-profit sector where she worked in public relations, program design, social media, grant writing and development.

Although now separated, Angel enjoyed a 20-year marriage to poet Darrell Parry who proved pivotal to bringing Angel's fiction writing career to fruition. Angel and Darrell both have disabilities. Angel had mild cerebral palsy which she has embarked on a journey to understand more about. Darrell has a club hand. They have an able-bodied teen daughter, Eva, who keeps bringing home strays — leaving them with a current count of four cats, one pit bull/black lab/mastiff puppy, one goffin cockatoo, one parakeet and multiple foster cats from their volunteer work with Feline Urban Rescue and Rehab.

Angel holds a bachelor's degree in English Language and Literature and French from Moravian College, a bachelor's in International Affairs (with honors) from Lafayette College, and initiated a master's degree in World History at West Chester University. Her academic interests include French post-colonial Africa, Muslim relations, and the politics of miscegenation. She hopes to revisit her honors thesis which looked at the stereotypes of Muslims in France and how they continue the thought process of the colonial era. The update would encourage readers to compare the attitudes of European Imperialism to modern race/minority relations.

In addition to Lehigh Valley, Pa., newspapers, Angel has been published in *Ten Word Stories* by *Dime Show Review, Rum Punch Press, StepAway Magazine,* two volumes of *The SAGE Encyclopedia,* and did book reviews for *Hippocampus Magazine* and *Journal of Global South Studies.*

When not examining the world with a post-colonial critical theorist's eye, Angel loves to travel and study foreign languages. She has visited Canada, France, Tunisia, Somalia, Djibouti, Yemen and various parts of Russia (such as trekking to Siberia for pizza). Read more of her escapades at AngelAckerman.com and follow her on YouTube, LinkedIn and Instagram.

BOOK 1: MANIPULATIONS

Weirdness surrounds Adelaide Pitney, former house model at Parisian fashion house Chez d'Amille. It always has. When she meets Galen Sorbach, an aspiring photographer, she hopes she's found a normal boyfriend, for once. She doesn't realize that Galen has been stalking her for latent healing powers, water magick she's used accidentally in large quantities. A fire mage, Galen never mastered water magick. Adelaide's gifts could be the power he needs to depose the Spirit Guardian and become a god.

Galen's sister, Kait, has spent 400 years as the elemental water guardian. Assigned to subdue Adelaide's magick, Kait delays. Her reluctance allows Galen to manipulate Adelaide and threatens the safety of the person Adelaide loves most, couturier Étienne d'Amille, and his lover, Basilie.

These five people — a 400-year-old Irish witch, her adopted psychopathic brother, an American supermodel, a French fashion designer, and his rich ex-wife — find their lives intertwined as they explore how far they will go for love and how much they can forgive.

—— E X C E R P T ——

August 2002

CHAPTER ONE

Lughaidh gripped the crumpled *People* magazine page against the steering wheel as he stared across the parking lot. It had been too easy to track her. A supermodel should know better. He relaxed his fingers and the page drifted to reveal photographs of fashion designer Étienne d'Amille's renovated farmhouse, one particular photo and caption circled with a thick black marker. In it, Adelaide Pitney arranged pottery in a mustard-gold painted kitchen with, if Lughaidh could trust the photograph, Tiger's Eye countertops. The caption read:

"D'Amille's long-time muse helped him find many of the distinctive elements of the home, situated in Upper Mount Bethel Township on River Road."

That provided enough information. Lughaidh found Adelaide and waited for her to leave without the French boss. After a trip to a grocery store twelve miles away, she'd led him to this dumpy bar. Someone even partially famous should have been harder to track, but Adelaide Pitney didn't act like a celebrity. You'd think she'd be more careful. You'd think she'd travel with someone. You never know when someone might pop out of the bushes with a razor and cut that beautiful face.

Lughaidh reached for his cigarettes. The styrofoam cup where he stored his cigarette butts had gone from empty to full during this recent hunt. Snapping his thumb against his index finger, Lughaidh conjured a flame from his finger-tip and lit his smoke. Fire could mar Adelaide's flawless skin. The flame on his finger died. Lughaidh inhaled and watched her, as he had for the last several days.

BOOK 2: COURTING APPARITIONS

World famous fashion designer Étienne d'Amille knows he should be grateful. He's survived several personal tragedies and almost died. He and his ex-wife, Zélie, will welcome their first born child into the world after 20 years of infertility. But grief has crippled Étienne. And his depression has threatened his relationships. So many questions linger about recent events: Did he take advantage of his protégé/supermodel Adelaide Pitney? Did he miss warning signs that could have prevented everything? And when Étienne's just about to crack—he discovers his house is haunted and the ghost stuck there begs him to free it before familiar supernatural creatures kill them all. Did Étienne receive the second chance he wanted? Or will he plunge into a magickal universe he's not equipped to understand?

—— E X C E R P T ——

CHAPTER ONE

É tienne d'Amille clung to the steering wheel of his wife's Mercedes, his fingers' grip stretching the leather of his favorite driving gloves. The keys laid in his lap as he surveyed the parking lot from his rear view mirror. The typical array of dusty pickup trucks, Chevrolets and Fords surrounded him except for one gleaming black sports car with white racing stripes.

A Dodge Viper. His eyes remained nailed to the spot. Or, how did the Americans put it? Glued. Glued to the spot. The heavy emptiness inside him since September now ached, even worse than inside the house.

He couldn't sleep inside the house. He hadn't gone into the bathroom where Adelaide committed suicide, where he had his heart attack, but yet his wife slept in the next room. He couldn't. But then, these days he barely slept anywhere… Not in Paris, not in Manhattan and certainly not here in rural Pennsylvania.

He thought he would sneak to the bar, have a beer, and go home. This tiny town had a population of 400 people and in that respect, it reminded him of the French countryside. Not much to do and not much there. This particular hamlet had one option at this advanced hour of the night: a bar péquenot… peasant? Redneck? He hadn't expected to find anyone he knew, or anyone who knew him, let alone the Viper.

Galen's Viper. The aspiring photographer had dated Adelaide. She was completely infatuated with him. Étienne hadn't heard of him or seen him since her death. Of course, Étienne hadn't been in the United States… His gaze shifted from the reflection of the parking lot onto his own eyes, their color partially hidden by his blond bangs. He brushed the curls from his face, touching the wrinkles in his forehead that had grown deeper in recent months. He took the keys from his lap and climbed from the car, his left leg protesting as he stood and retrieved his cane. The golden S600 chirped as he locked it with the fob and slipped the keys into his pocket. He slowly approached the bar, the gravel crunchy and uneven under his feet.

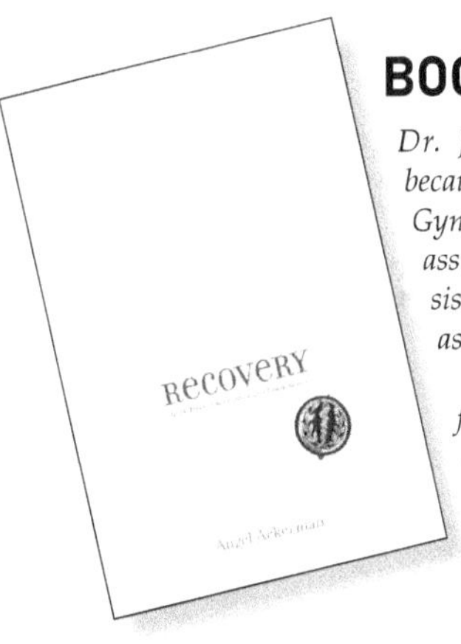

BOOK 3: RECOVERY

Dr. Jacqueline Saint-Ebène joined the French Defense Health Service because she had grown bored of vaginas. But neither her years as an Ob-Gyn nor her tour as a combat surgeon in Africa prepared her for her latest assignment: a supernatural immaculate conception, her pregnant oldest sister's stroke, and the army's concern that her brother-in-law might exist as the center of it all.

While Jacqueline grapples with family and military drama, she also finds herself in a personal crisis in Djibouti. She underestimated the role of Issa Somali culture in her boyfriend's life and learns he has a secret that threatens the core of their relationship.

Throw in a sexy young werewolf—and, yes, werewolves are real — and Jacqueline doesn't know where to find the truth.

—— EXCERPT ——

CHAPTER ONE

Hoisting her pregnant older sister, a stroke victim with limited use of her right side, into the cabin of a Falcon jet had proven the most grueling challenge of Jacqueline Saint-Ebène's career as a military doctor. By the time she cajoled Basilie's uncooperative body up the stairs, Jacqueline thought her own arms might fall off. Somehow, Jacqueline managed to guide Basilie into the leather chair across from the door and buckle her seatbelt for her. Basilie offered a weak smile, the effort as exhausting for her as it had been for Jacqueline, and muttered 'maan.' Jacqueline tucked her shoulder-length hair behind her ears as she met her sister's gaze.

"You're welcome," she said in their native French.

Since the stroke two weeks ago, speech therapy had returned a few words to Basilie. 'Maan' was the attempt at the French word for 'thank you,' 'merci.' Basilie laid her hand against a German economics book on the table, something about the new Euro currency and its impact on the financial markets from what Jacqueline could translate. German never interested Jacqueline nor did economics. Basilie opened the paperback and read.

The men boarded the plane. Jacqueline had requested time to settle Basilie so her sister wouldn't be embarrassed by her lack of mobility. Basilie's ex-husband, fashion designer Étienne d'Amille, brushed by them, taking the seat opposite Basilie. Étienne kissed his ex-wife's forehead as he passed. Étienne's former army buddy and current business second-in-command, Didier Robineau, claimed the chair on the other side of the aisle, fastening the lap belt which disappeared beneath his tweed blazer.

Jules Zweigenbaum, Étienne's private chef, a tall, long-haired fellow who'd spent his youth surfing in Berritz and had the body to show for it, entered the plane next to last, leaving only Doctor-in-Chief Philomé Abdullahi on the tarmac. Jules went to the rear of the plane sitting to the left of the lavatory on the aisle seat. He stretched across the seat beside him and closed the window shade.

Additional Titles From

Parisian Phoenix
PUBLISHING

AVAILABLE NOW

at your independent bookseller or online at

barnesandnoble.com, amazon.com, and bookshop.org.

TRAPPED by Seneca Blue

Edna Gardner, who goes by Ed, is overeducated and and underemployed, approaching 40 and overweight. She hasn't had a date in several presidential administrations, works several part-time jobs (professor, graphic designer, photographer and journalist among them), and has resigned herself to a future with her drunken sister, Gertrude, as a roommate in the dying steel town where they were born. Her life consists of one comedic tragedy after another, until the day skunks invade her backyard. Then, she hires Clint Anderson to trap her skunks, and he revives her interest in men, builds her confidence and shows her that maybe she can fall in love.

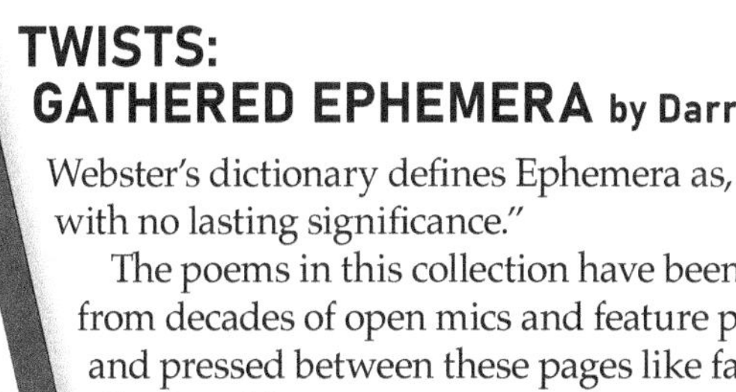

TWISTS:
GATHERED EPHEMERA by Darrell Parry

Webster's dictionary defines Ephemera as, "something with no lasting significance."

The poems in this collection have been swept together from decades of open mics and feature performances, and pressed between these pages like fallen leaves as fleeting things, now preserved.

This book, complete with nifty drawings and sage bits of wisdom scattered throughout, offers a glimpse into a world of social anxiety and awkwardness with the experience and wisdom to accept an epic unknowing of everything.

STOPS ALONG THE WAY by Charles Ticho

In this unique autobiographical collection of essays, highly influenced by his experiences during World War II, nonagenarian Charles Ticho documents his and his family's life during the Holocaust in what is now the Czech Republic. With the innocence of a child, he explores his journey through Europe to the United States, explaining how his family survived and started over. The book follows Charles into his career in film production and to present-day Israel. This heart-warming book documents a troubled period of twentieth century history and chronicles one Jewish family's legacy.